I WAS JUST ABOUT...

BY MARK H. MCCRAW

ILLUSTRATED BY MEAGHAN MCCRAW-TEAL

PALMETTO
PUBLISHING

Charleston, SC
www.PalmettoPublishing.com

I Was Just About...
Copyright © 2022 by Mark H. McCraw

First Edition

Hardcover ISBN: 979-8-9858936-4-9
Paperback ISBN: 979-8-9858936-5-6
eBook ISBN: 979-8-9858936-6-3

This book is dedicated to my son Mark II.

I was just about…
to enjoy my friends.

12
3
6
9
SCHOOL

I was just about…
to enjoy my school.

I was just about…
to enjoy my house.

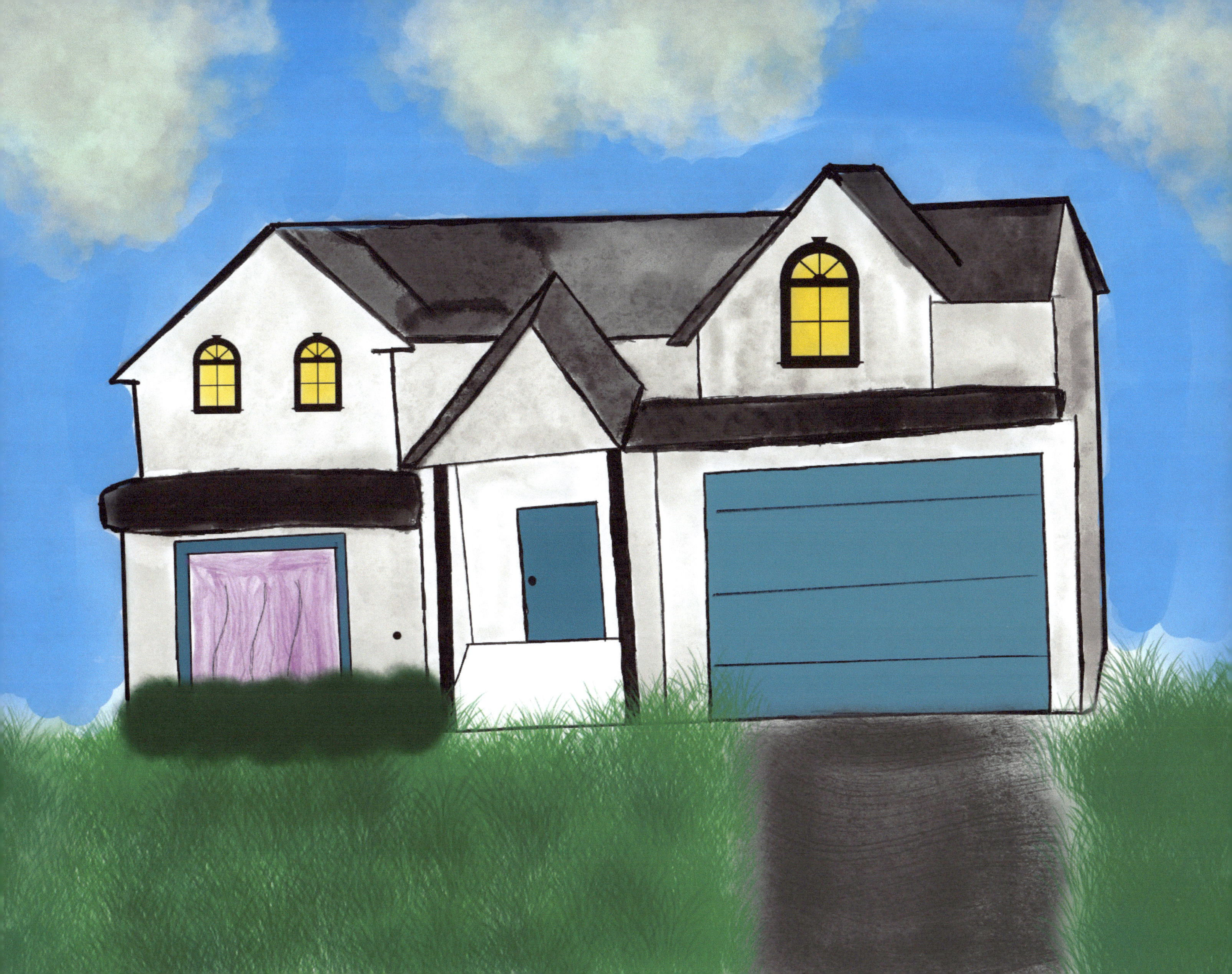

I was just about…
to enjoy my city.

Then my dad told us the news.

We are moving again!

Oh, No!

I know everything will be okay
even though we are packing today.
I will find a new place
with a larger space
and friends I will meet at school.
So that is cool.

For at first, I thought I was in despair
and life was not fair.
But now I must prepare…

for a new place with new friends.